...ly going to give it a t...

sai...

...cided to start that very day. Afte... ...ch
tho... ...e composed something to say las... ...g at
nigh... ...d.

H... ...e a simple request to start wi... ...s he
felt ... ...self drifting off to sleep, he said...

'Tomorrow what I'm wanting m...
...s something for me in the pos...

Also by Dick King-Smith from Young Hippo:

What Sadie Saw

Uncle Bumpo

Bobby the Bad

Warlock Watson

Dick King-Smith

Hippo

Scholastic Children's Books,
Commonwealth House, 1-19 New Oxford Street,
London, WC1A 1NU, UK
A division of Scholastic Ltd
London ~ New York ~ Toronto ~ Sydney ~ Auckland
Mexico City ~ New Delhi ~ Hong Kong

First published by Scholastic Ltd, 1995
This edition, 1999

ISBN 0590 13366 7

Typeset by DP Photosetting, Aylesbury, Bucks
Printed by Mackays of Chatham plc, Chatham, Kent

10 9 8 7 6 5 4 3 2 1

Contents

1 The Postcard   7

2 The Knife   13

3 The Washing-machine   23

4 The Accident   31

5 The Match   40

6 The Thunderstorm   50

7 The Gypsy   58

8 The Cypress   69

9 The Final Rhyme   79

Chapter 1

The Postcard

Sam looked up from his book.

"Mum," he said. "What's a warlock?"

"A sort of wizard," his mother said. "Like a witch, only a man. Witches are female, warlocks are male. They can do magic."

"Not half!" said Sam. "The one in this story just pushed a big tree down. He didn't have an axe or a saw or anything; he just put his hand against the tree and said,

'Tree so tall
Fall, tree, fall!'

And it did!"

"Wow!" said his mother. "Some warlock!"

Sam, sitting at the kitchen table, read on for a while

in silence while his mother got on with some cooking. Then he said, "Mum."

"Yes?"

"How d'you get to be one?"

"To be what?"

"A warlock."

"Well, you can't just get to be one," Sam's mother said. "It isn't like saying, 'I'm going to be a motor mechanic' or 'I'm going to be a plumber.' You can't simply decide to be a warlock. It isn't something you can learn to be."

"I wish I could," said Sam. "This one's built a house out of that tree already. He didn't have to saw it up into beams and planks and stuff; he just said some magic rhymes and – hey presto! There was his house. Why, just think, Mum, if I was a warlock, you wouldn't ever have to do any more cooking. I'd just say something like,

> 'We'll have fish and chips for tea,
> Fish for you and chips for me.'

and there they'd be, on the table."

"What about Dad? Doesn't he get any?"

"Oh, sorry. Let's see now...

     'Here's another wish.

     Extra chips and fish

     For my dad, of course,

     With tomato sauce.'"

"Dad doesn't like tomato sauce."

"No, but I do," said Sam. "And just think, Mum; you wouldn't have to do any housework – no dusting or cleaning or hoovering – and you wouldn't have to do the washing. You wouldn't even need to go shopping; you could tell me what you wanted and I'd say a magic rhyme and all the food and stuff would just arrive."

"That'd save a lot of money," his mother said.

"Oh, you wouldn't have to worry about money," said Sam. "You could have all you wanted, and Dad could retire, I'd be making so much money."

"Earning it, d'you mean?" asked his mother.

"No! Just making it. By magic. Ten-pound notes, twenty-pound notes, fifty-pound notes... Some pound coins, I suppose, but nothing smaller. I should think that would be simple for a warlock."

"Sounds lovely. I wish you were one."

"I'll see what I can do," said Sam. He read on.

By the end of the story the warlock had got all the things he wanted – a house, a wife, a carriage drawn by six snow-white horses, and a pair of fur-lined boots – just by making up a few simple rhymes.

"Becoming a warlock's as easy as pie.

If that's how he does it, then why shouldn't I?

I'm certainly going to give it a try,"
said Sam.

He decided to start that very day. After much thought, he composed something to say last thing at night in bed.

He chose a simple request to start with. Just as he felt himself drifting off to sleep, he said,

"Tomorrow what I'm wanting most

Is something for me in the post."
He'd picked this because if it worked, it would be a minor miracle. Sam never wrote letters to anyone so he never received any.

As soon as he woke next morning he hurried downstairs to see if the postman had been. He had. There was a pile of letters on the mat.

Sam looked through them. Four were for Dad (Mr J. Watson) – bills, by the look of them. One was for Mum (Mrs J. Watson). There were two circulars (for Mr and Mrs J. Watson) and, last of all, a postcard. It was addressed to Sam Watson, c/o Mr and Mrs J. Watson.

Fantastic! thought Sam. It worked! He turned it over. It was from the local library. It said,

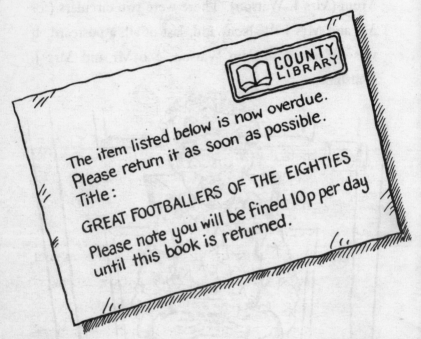

COUNTY LIBRARY

The item listed below is now overdue. Please return it as soon as possible.

Title:

GREAT FOOTBALLERS OF THE EIGHTIES

Please note you will be fined 10p per day until this book is returned.

Chapter 2
The Knife

After school that day, Sam went to the library with his mother. He handed in *Great Footballers of the Eighties*. She handed over the fine.

Sam chose another book.

"If you forget to return this one," his mother said, "you can pay next time. What have you got, anyway?"

"*Witchcraft*," said Sam.

That evening, he hurried through his homework and then settled down with the new book.

"Anything in it about warlocks?" his mother asked.

"Warlocks?" said his father.

"Not much," Sam said.

"Sam wants to be one," his mother said.

"Then it's a good job you didn't live a few hundred

years ago," said his father.

"Why?"

"They used to throw people into rivers if they suspected them of being witches or warlocks. If they drowned, then they weren't."

"And if they floated?"

"That proved they were witches. So they hanged them."

"Warlocks too?"

"Yes. There was a famous 'witch-finder' called Matthew Hopkins who hanged sixty witches in one year. And in the end he was chucked in too and he floated, so they strung him up."

Sam thought about this. After a while he said, "I can swim, anyway," but no one answered because they had switched on the television.

Sam closed *Witchcraft* with a sigh. Silly little book, he thought. It's all about witches and broomsticks and black cats and stuff. Doesn't really say anything much about warlocks, and nothing about magic rhymes. But I *did* say one last night and I *did* get something in the post. Not many people could do that, I bet. Mum and

Dad would be pretty amazed if they knew.

And when it was time for bed and his father said, "Goodnight, Warlock Watson," he just smiled. You wait, he said to himself. I just might be.

Over the following few days, Sam spent some time trying to decide what the next magic rhyme should be. Asking for something in the post was about as humble a wish as you could make. And it wasn't Christmas for ages and it was nowhere near his birthday, so there wasn't much point in trying for a computer or a synthesizer or something big like that. What, then?

I know, he thought. I had an old penknife but I lost it. It was a rotten old thing anyway, so blunt it would hardly sharpen a pencil. I'd like another. A decent one, what's more; perhaps a Swiss Army sort with two blades and a corkscrew and a thing for getting stones out of horses' hooves. Though, come to think of it, I suppose a warlock wouldn't actually need a penknife. He'd be able to cut things and make corks pop out of bottles and stones drop out of horses' hooves by magic. Still, I want one.

Let's see ... what rhymes with "knife"? "Life"? "Wife"? That's no good. I'll have to do it differently.

He thought for a bit and then cried, "Got it!" and said, slowly and clearly,

"I want a knife. No ifs or buts.

I want a knife that really cuts."

The simplest way for his new knife to come, Sam supposed, would be through the post. There'd be a little parcel addressed to him and inside, there it would be. Warlocks just commanded something to happen and it did.

But it didn't.

Each day, in the privacy of his bedroom, Sam repeated the magic rhyme, but no parcel came, and no one offered to buy him a new knife. And I'm not going to use my pocket money to get one, said Sam to himself. Warlocks don't buy things; they don't have to.

About a week later, however, the postman brought a letter addressed to "Mr and Mrs J. Watson" that caused them some excitement. It was from a friend whom they hadn't seen for a long time. He'd been working abroad, and wrote to say he would be passing through and could he come and see them?

"You've never met Phil, have you, Sam?" said his father.

"Who's Phil?"

"He's an old friend of Dad's," Sam's mother said. "Actually, he's your godfather, though he's never done much about that, but then he's been working in South America ever since you were very small."

"You'll like old Phil," Sam's father said.

I might, thought Sam, and I might not. Grown-ups seem to think that just because they like someone, you will too.

But in fact when this unknown godfather turned up for a meal a couple of days later, Sam thought he was nice. He told lots of stories about his life as an engineer in Brazil, and he seemed interested in Sam and didn't talk down to him.

When he was about to go, Phil said, "I should have brought you a present, godson Sam, but I forgot."

He fished around in his pocket as though searching for money, and then he said, "I know! Would you like this?" and he pulled out a small black leather case.

"What is it?" said Sam.

Phil undid a button that kept the case closed and drew out a chunky little penknife with a handle made of wood and brass.

"I bought this one day in Rio," he said, "and, d'you know, I've never actually used it, so it's as good as new. It's only got the one blade but there's a special spring that locks the blade open, like this. Then you press down the spring to close it. Would you like it?"

"Oh, yes, please!" said Sam. I do believe I *am* a warlock, he thought.

"You must give me a coin," said Phil.

"Why?"

"If you give someone a knife without being paid for it, it cuts a friendship. Any coin. A penny will do."

Sam handed over a penny and Phil handed over the little knife, buttoned up in its leather case.

"Oh, thanks!" Sam said. "Thanks a million!"

After his godfather had gone, Sam went out into the garden to admire his new knife. Magic! he thought. I can do magic!

He took it out of its case and clicked open the

pointed blade. How shiny and new-looking it was. How sharp it looked.

He picked up a small branch that was lying on the ground and began to whittle it. How easily the blade sliced through the wood! Then his hand slipped and the blade sliced deep into his left thumb and the blood came spurting out.

"Mum! Dad! I'm bleeding to death!" shouted Sam, rushing into the house.

"You'll have to have a couple of stitches in that," said the doctor when he saw it. "How did you do it?"

"With my new knife," Sam said.

"Hmm," said the doctor. "One thing's sure: you've got a knife that really cuts."

Chapter 3
The Washing-machine

"Well, you've learned two lessons recently, haven't you?" said Sam's mother.

"How d'you mean?"

"Remember to return library books in time, and be careful with sharp knives."

"And don't," said Sam's father, "go mixing up any magic potions."

"Why should I?"

"Well, that's what people like you do, isn't it, Warlock Watson? You'd probably poison someone."

"I'm not going to be that sort of warlock," Sam said.

"Oh. I see."

You will, Sam thought. You will. I'll get it right. I've just had a bit of bad luck so far. Perhaps it's because

I've been a bit selfish, just wanting things for myself – something in the post, then a penknife. I'll try magicking things for Mum and Dad.

So – ladies first. What would Mum like?

He wandered into the utility room where the washing-machine was humming away. We've had that quite a long time, he thought. I'm sure she'd like a new one.

The machine shut itself off, just as his mother came in.

"Mum," said Sam, "wouldn't you like a new washing-machine?"

"No, thanks. This one's fine."

"We've had it a long time."

"Only a couple of years. These things go on for ages."

All the same, said Sam to himself later, I bet you wouldn't mind a brand-new one, a really modern model. That would be a real test of my warlockry. I'll see what I can do.

He spent some time trying in vain to find a rhyme for "washing-machine", and then a new idea struck him. I'll just say a magic rhyme to the thing, he thought, and see what happens.

Making sure his mother was busy elsewhere, Sam went back into the utility room and stood beside the washing-machine. Then he said (loudly to make himself heard above its hum):

"I want a new machine for Mum
For her to do the washing.
Your time is up. The moment's come
For you to stop your sloshing."

For a few seconds the machine hummed on happily, and then suddenly there was an explosive noise inside it – an awful metallic grinding and crashing as though it were full, not of clothes, but of knives and spoons and forks all being ground up into little bits. Sam smelled smoke, and a thin wisp of it rose into the air. Then there was silence.

His mother came rushing in. "What was that noise?" she cried.

"Dunno," said Sam. "It's stopped," he added.

"Well, I can see that, you stupid boy! What did you do to it?"

"I never touched it, Mum!" said Sam. "Honest I didn't."

His mother opened the lid and peered in, and then began pressing various buttons, but nothing happened.

"Whatever's wrong with the thing?" she said angrily. "Right in the middle of a big wash too. It's never given a moment's trouble before."

"Perhaps something's bust," said Sam.

His mother looked at him narrowly for a moment. Then she went off to make a phone call.

"It just stopped, you say?" asked Sam's father that evening.

"Yes," his wife said. "It made a horrible crashing, clashing noise right in the middle of a wash. I got the man out to look at it and he says it's a write-off, not worth the expense of trying to repair it. The motor's burned out and all the bearings have stripped or something – I couldn't understand what he was saying. He's never known such a thing happen to any sort of washing-machine ever before."

"And of course it's no longer under guarantee," said Sam's father.

"No," said his mother, "and we talked about insuring it, remember?"

"But we never did."

"It means a new one."

"What will that cost? Did you ask?"

"Yes. Five hundred pounds."

"Whew!" said Sam, despite himself.

"Funny thing," his mother said to her husband. "Not half an hour before it broke down, Sam asked me whether I would like a new one, didn't you, Sam?"

Sam nodded.

His father looked narrowly at him for a moment. Then he went off to make a phone call.

Sam lay in bed that night, thinking.

I didn't take enough trouble with that rhyme, he said to himself. I should have said something about getting a new washing-machine free. Now I've let them in for five hundred pounds.

Wait a minute, though! I can put that right! It's a lot

of money to Mum and Dad, but it's peanuts to a warlock. Let's see ... what shall I say?

Trying unsuccessfully to think of a rhyme, Sam fell asleep. But when he woke next morning, one was ready-formed in his head, and before even getting out of bed, he said,

"I need five hundred pounds without delay.
See that my mother's given it today."

By now Sam was becoming quite confident that his magic rhymes would do the trick, however it came about, and he was eating his breakfast, having almost

forgotten about the latest one, when his mother gave a shriek.

"Whatever's the matter?" said his father.

"I went in for a silly competition," said his mother, "in a magazine. First prize was a trip to Disneyland in Florida, but there were cash prizes too, and I've won one! Look! A cheque for five hundred pounds!"

"Five hundred pounds?" said Sam's father. "Why, that's the exact price..."

"...of a new washing-machine!" finished his mother.

"Gosh!" Sam said. "What a funny thing."

Chapter 4
The Accident

On Sam's bedroom wall was a small, square mirror. His mother had fixed it there in the hope that it would encourage him to comb his hair. This was a vain hope, since Sam only ever ran his fingers through his tousled mop.

Lately, however, he had taken to standing in front of the mirror and looking carefully at his reflection. Did warlocks look different from other people? If so, how? Funny teeth? Slitty eyes? Pointed ears?

He studied his reflection. It looked quite ordinary.

"But you're not," he said to it. "Ordinary, I mean. Just look at what you've done recently. What next? Well, it's Dad's turn, isn't it? I expect he'd like a new car, but then remember what happened to Mum's

washing-machine. We don't want all the wheels dropping off when he's whizzing along the motorway. Probably best to ask Mum what he'd like and then get it for him, don't you think?"

He nodded and his reflection nodded back.

He went to consult his mother.

"How's the new washing-machine, Mum?" he said.

"Fine. You keep away from it though."

"Why?"

"The only time you went near the old one, it fell to bits. Maybe washing-machines don't like warlocks. Or have you given up the idea?"

"What idea?"

"Of becoming a warlock."

Sam grinned. "You'd be surprised if I really was one, wouldn't you?" he said.

"I certainly would, and so would your father. Mind you, it could be very useful. You could make all sorts of wishes come true."

"What would Dad wish for, d'you think?" Sam said.

"A bit of a holiday, I should think," his mother said. "He's been under a lot of pressure at work and it's time he had a break."

No problem, Sam thought.

At school that morning Sam sat staring out of the classroom window, thinking of rhymes for "break".

"Sam Watson!" his teacher called. "Get on with your work."

Work, thought Sam, bending over his maths book. If only we didn't all have to work all the time. There's

Dad having to drive into the office every morning through all the traffic, and do whatever it is he does (Mr Watson was in insurance) all day long and then drive back again. And there's Mum having to do the housework and the shopping and all that gardening. (The Watsons had a large allotment and Mrs Watson did most of the work on it, selling surplus vegetables at a market stall.) And then there's me, having to do all this schoolwork, and homework on top of it. It isn't right. Warlocks shouldn't have to.

Anyway, I must see what I can fix for Dad.

He took a loose sheet of paper and began to write. Five minutes later Sam looked up to see Mr Hogg, his teacher, staring at him, and he hastily slipped the sheet of paper under his exercise book and began to copy out a sum.

Mr Hogg came to stand beside him.

"What are you doing, Sam?" he said.

"Maths, sir," Sam said.

The teacher picked up the exercise book and found

the piece of paper underneath. On it was written:

bake – cake – lake – make – rake – wake

"What's all this?" he said.

"I was just thinking of some rhymes," said Sam.

"I didn't know you were a poet, Sam," said Mr Hogg.

No, and you don't know I'm a warlock either, thought Sam.

"But," said Mr Hogg, "I can think of another word that rhymes with that lot. Which is 'break'."

Sam was about to say, "That's the word I need rhymes for" when the teacher went on, "And when it's time for break this morning, the rest of the class will go out and enjoy themselves in the playground while you, Sam Watson, do two pages of sums out of your maths problems books. And you'd better get them right."

He took the piece of paper and scrumpled it up and dropped it in the wastepaper bin.

"You'd better watch it," Sam said under his breath. "It isn't wise to tangle with Warlock Watson. 'Hogg' rhymes with 'frog', you know. You'd look pretty silly hopping into the Staff Room."

That evening Sam's father arrived home from work and flopped into a chair.

"Traffic bad?" asked Sam's mother.

"Terrible. And this morning too. And we're snowed under with work in the office – it's all these claims for damage after those bad storms. I'm worn out."

"I was only saying to Sam this morning," his wife said, "that you need a break, a clean break from work.

A fortnight, say, so that you could have a rest, a nice relaxing time."

"Great idea," said Sam's father, "but it's just not possible."

Oh, yes it is, thought Sam. He put what his mother had said into his own words and, shutting himself in his bedroom, spoke them solemnly.

"I want my Dad to have a break,
A rest, a nice relaxing time.
A fortnight's holiday he'll take
Because I say this magic rhyme."

Sam was slightly surprised when, next morning, his father drove off to work as usual.

But he was even more surprised, when he arrived home from school that afternoon, to find his next-door neighbour waiting for him.

"Oh, Sam!" she said. "Your mum's had to go out. She asked me to look after you till she gets back."

"Where's she gone?" Sam asked.

"To the hospital. Your dad's had a bit of an accident. They're plastering him up."

"Plastering him?"

"Yes, his right arm. He tripped up at work, fell down some stairs, and he's broken it. A nice clean break, they say, but he'll be off work for a couple of weeks."

Chapter 5
The Match

For the next couple of weeks Sam laid off warlockry. It seemed that his magic rhymes did funny things. He'd have to be more careful.

Meanwhile he returned *Witchcraft* to the library in good time, he used Phil's penknife with caution, he kept away from the new washing-machine, and he made an unusual fuss of his father.

In fact Mr Watson was thoroughly enjoying his unexpected break. His arm no longer hurt, he was unable to write anything, and he couldn't help with housework or shopping or gardening. He sat comfortably in his armchair, watching sport on TV.

His wife not only brought him his meals but cut them up for him, and his son seemed strangely anxious

about his welfare, constantly asking if he was all right
and whether there was anything he wanted.

"What's up with Sam?" his father said. "He keeps
asking how my arm feels and saying how sorry he is
that I broke it. Anyone would think it was his fault."

"What's that written on your plaster?" said his wife.

Her husband held up his arm.

In red felt-tip pen were the words,

GET WELL SOON

(sighned) WARLOCK WATSON

"Warlocks may be able to cast spells, but they can't spell," she said.

"I'm not sure that I want to get well soon," Sam's father said, pressing the remote control of the TV. "Ah, good. Racing at Ascot. Could I have another mug of coffee? And some of those shortbread biscuits, please? By the way, what's for supper?"

After much thought, Sam decided that his next attempt at magic should not involve the family, but someone else. Who, though? Someone at school? Piggy? (This of course was what the children called Mr Hogg behind his broad back. He did look a bit like one.)

No, Piggy wasn't too bad really. He didn't deserve to be turned into a frog, and anyway, Sam said to himself, I don't think I'm that sort of a warlock; I'd rather try to do nice things for people. There are good fairies and wicked fairies, and nice witches and nasty ones. I'm a good warlock, I am.

Sam's friend Ben made his mind up for him.

Ben was crazy about football. He had a book filled with stickers of all the Premier League teams, and he knew the name of almost every player. Though smaller than Sam, he was a promising footballer. He was very quick about the pitch, his control of the ball was good, and he could kick with either foot.

Ben longed to play for the school First Eleven, and one day his dream came true. One of the regular players was away ill on the eve of a match against a neighbouring school, and Mr Hogg, who was in charge of games, called up Ben.

Ben lost no time in telling Sam.

"What d'you think, Sam?" he said. "Piggy's picked me to play for the school this afternoon, on the wing! I'll be the youngest player on our side, he said."

"Brilliant!" Sam said.

"All this term," Ben said, "I've been hoping and hoping I might get into the side but I never thought I would, not till next year anyway."

Silly me, thought Sam. I could have fixed that for you weeks ago.

"Wouldn't it be great," said Ben, "if I could score the winning goal!"

Now that, thought Sam, I can fix.

"You will, Ben," he said. "You will."

Ben laughed. "Fat chance!" he said. "You coming to watch?"

"Wouldn't miss it," said Sam.

And nor will you, he thought, I'll see to that. I've just got to make sure I get the words right this time – don't want Ben scoring an own goal. And I mustn't write any rhymes down in class – don't want Piggy after me again.

Sam decided to wait until the end of the day to compose his next magic rhyme. In the afternoon – for the last quarter of an hour or so – Mr Hogg always read his class a story to finish the day with. That should give me time, thought Sam.

And so it did. By the time the teacher closed the book, Sam had his rhyme ready in his head.

He kept a little way apart from the other children as they made their way over to the playing-field, and quietly chanted,

"I want our football team to win.
I want them to and so they will.
And Ben will knock the winner in
To make the final score One-Nil."
He heard heavy footsteps behind him and Mr Hogg
caught him up. He seemed in a jolly mood.

"Enjoy the story today, did you, Sam?" he asked.

"Oh, yes, sir," Sam said.

Oh, Lor'! he thought. What was it about? I never listened to a word.

"I like stories about magic, don't you?" said Piggy. He was wearing a pink track suit, ready to referee the match, and he looked more than ever like a big fat porker.

"Oh, yes," said Sam. "Do you believe in magic, sir?"

"I believe that sometimes things happen that we can't easily explain."

"Like someone saying that something's going to happen, and then it does happen?"

"Prophesy, you mean?" said Mr Hogg. "Foretelling the future?"

"Yes, sir," said Sam. "Like if I said to you, 'We're going to win the match today.'"

"Well, that's an even money chance, like calling heads or tails."

"What if I said, 'We'll win One-Nil'?"

"That's just a guess."

"Well, suppose I said, 'We'll win One-Nil, and Ben will be the scorer'?"

Mr Hogg laughed, and gave Sam a friendly pat on the back that almost knocked him flat.

"Your friend Ben, scoring the winning goal on his first appearance for the school? That would be magic, Sam, that would!" he said, and he broke into a heavy-footed run.

"It will be, Piggy," said Sam.

When the match started, it would have been plain to anyone with a knowledge of football that neither team was particularly good. There was an awful lot of aimless kicking and wild passes and dramatic falls, but it never looked as if either side was capable of scoring a goal, and indeed at half-time there was no score.

In the second half the visitors hit the woodwork once, and once the home team put the ball in their opponents' net, but Mr Hogg blew for offside.

With only a few minutes of time left, the game seemed destined to be a goalless draw. Then, just as Mr Hogg was looking at his watch, there was a goalmouth scramble right in front of the visitors' posts. The goalie was off his line and on the ground along with several others, attackers and defenders, when suddenly the ball came loose, and little Ben, appearing at high speed from nowhere, popped it into the undefended net. A

loud blast from Piggy's whistle signified the end of the
game and victory for the home team, One-Nil.

As players and referee trooped off the pitch, Sam
caught Mr Hogg's eye.

"Sir! Sir!" he cried. "That was magic, wasn't it?"

Chapter 6
The Thunderstorm

When Sam arrived in his classroom next morning, Mr Hogg beckoned to him.

"Tell me, Sam," he said, "do you have any Scottish blood? Watson is a Scottish name, as indeed is Hogg."

"A bit, sir," Sam said. "One of my great-grand-fathers, I think it was, came from Scotland."

"From the Highlands?"

"I don't know, sir. Why?"

"Highlanders sometimes have the gift of second sight. Maybe you've inherited it. Otherwise what you said to me yesterday on our way over to the playing field takes a bit of explaining. 'We'll win One-Nil, and Ben will be the scorer,' you said, remember?"

"I remember," said Sam.

Mr Hogg looked narrowly at Sam out of his little piggy eyes. He shook his head and gave a sudden snorting laugh.

"Must be witchcraft," he said.

Sam smiled. "I couldn't be a witch, sir," he said. "Witches are female."

"In that case," grunted Piggy, with another snort of amusement, "you must be a warlock! We'll have to call you Warlock Watson."

The rest of the class were beginning to look up from their tables, wondering what was making Piggy laugh, and Sam said quickly, "I'd rather you didn't tell anyone, sir. They'll only take the mickey."

"Are you not going to tell Ben that you foresaw the result?"

"No, sir. I don't want anyone else to know."

There are people who can be trusted to keep secrets, and people who cannot keep them for love nor money. Mr Hogg was one of those who could.

"OK, Sam," he said. "I'll be like dad and keep mum. In return, you could do something for me."

"What?"

"Favour me with your attention when I read to you this afternoon. I had my eye on you yesterday. What you were thinking about I don't know, but you weren't listening to a single word I read. Off you go now." He took the class register from his desk.

"Answer your names," he said.

The names of the class were in alphabetical order, and "Sam Watson" was the last to be called.

"Here, sir," Sam answered. Thank goodness I asked

Piggy not to tell, he thought, or he'd probably have shouted out "Warlock Watson" and I'd never have heard the last of it.

At morning break out in the playground, Sam was kicking a ball about with Ben and a lot of other boys.

"You told me I'd score the winning goal, didn't you?" Ben shouted.

"Well, yes, I did," said Sam, "but I couldn't possibly have known you would, could I?"

"Course you couldn't," Ben said. "Not unless you were some sort of magician!"

I am, thought Sam. I can make things happen. It isn't seeing into the future like Piggy thinks; it's fixing what the future will bring. I mean, it may be going to rain tomorrow or it may not. But if I made up a rhyme telling it to rain tomorrow, then it would. And what's more, I bet I could pick the exact time it would start. And stop.

For example, he thought, I could say,

"Tomorrow it will simply pour

With rain from two o'clock till four."

Sam forgot about this till school had ended, and then on the way home he remembered it and, in an absentminded sort of way, actually spoke it out loud.

That evening, a Friday, Sam's father said to his wife, "I'm seeing the doctor tomorrow morning. If he says it's OK, I'll be starting work again on Monday. I've had a nice break."

"I just hope that it's fine tomorrow afternoon," said Sam's mother. Sam pricked up his ears.

"Why, Mum?" he said. "What's happening tomorrow?"

"It's the Women's Institute Autumn Fête. On the Recreation Ground. None of the stalls will be under cover, so we desperately need a fine afternoon."

"What time does it start?" Sam asked.

"Two o'clock. It's from two till four."

Oh, no! thought Sam. In his mind's eye he could see the rain teeming down and all the ladies getting soaked and all the produce being ruined and the whole thing being a disastrous wash-out – thanks to him!

How do I take back a magic rhyme? he said to himself, as he lay in bed that night. Just because I happened to pick on those times, Mum's fête's going to be totally messed up. I'll have to think up another rhyme cancelling the first one.

But somehow he simply couldn't think of one, try as he might. It was as though something was stopping him, and he fell asleep without succeeding.

When it was time for breakfast he was still asleep and his mother came to wake him.

"Nothing much disturbs you, does it?" she said.

"What d'you mean?" Sam mumbled.

"You never heard all that noise in the night?"

"What noise?"

"There was a tremendous thunderstorm – the heavens opened and it poured and poured with rain."

"Oh," said Sam. "What time was that?"

"It started at two and went on for a good couple of hours."

A.m.! thought Sam. Two a.m., not two p.m.! Now I should be able to fix this afternoon. While he was getting dressed, he made up the rhyme he needed.

"Now that the rain has gone away,

I want the sun to shine all day,"

he said. And it did.

"How did the fête go?" Sam's father asked his wife that evening.

"Wonderfully well," she said, "thanks to the weather – it might have been specially ordered. What a perfect autumn day it's been! Loads of people came and we've made a lot of money for charity."

"Charity begins at home," Sam's father said. "What's for supper? Sam and I are famished."

"I haven't had time to get anything ready, I'm

afraid. You'll just have to scrounge something."

Sam suddenly thought of those rhymes he'd made up when he was first talking to his mother about warlocks, and he ran out into the garden and said them. Then he heard his father's voice.

"Sam!" he called. "Come on – we'll go down to the chippy."

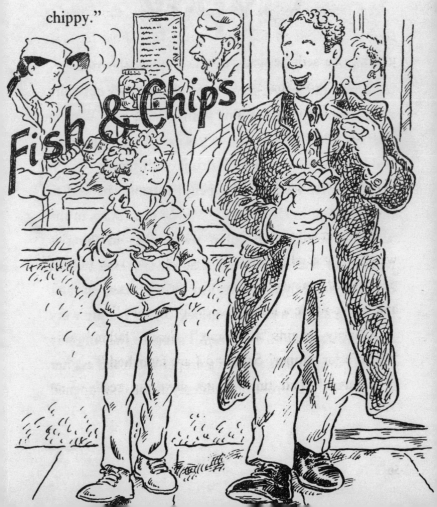

Chapter 7
The Gypsy

An older and wiser warlock would have learned by now that magic spells don't always work out quite as you thought. But at nine years of age, Sam Watson was not very old nor yet very wise. What's more, he had by now become a little drunk with power.

"Whatever I want to happen, happens," he said to his reflection in the mirror. "Maybe not always in the way I expected, but still it seems that anything is possible to Warlock Watson. I can do anything I like. I expect I could fly if I wanted to. Witches can, on their broomsticks, so maybe a warlock could. It didn't say anything about it in *Witchcraft*. I suppose the only way to find out would be to meet a proper witch and ask her whether —" He broke off suddenly as the door opened and his mother poked her head round it.

"Whatever are you rabbiting on about?" she said.

"Just talking to myself," said Sam.

"First sign of madness. Or is it something to do with being a warlock? Anyway, let's have your dirty clothes. I'm doing a wash this morning."

"In your new machine, paid for by Warlock Watson," said Sam, when she had gone.

At school that morning, Sam spent a lot of time thinking about this latest idea – to meet a witch and have a good talk about witchcraft and warlockry. There must still be witches about, even if nowadays they weren't always being thrown into rivers. How could you find one? You could hardly advertise.

> *Warlock (9) wishes to meet experienced witch*
> *(any age) to discuss matters of magic.*
> *Sam Watson, 23 Redbarrow Road.*

Not until Piggy had bawled him out several times for daydreaming did the obvious solution occur to him.

A magic rhyme, of course! I'll just order a witch to turn up and she will.

It didn't take Sam long to think up a rhyme, and after lunch he went off to a far corner of the playground by himself and said,

"A witch is what I want to find –
What kind of witch I do not mind –
To ask her whether it is right
That warlocks have the power of flight.
So listen, witch: do what I say.
I need you to appear today."

Walking home from school, Sam looked carefully at all the women he saw in the street. Any one of them could be a witch, I suppose, he thought. You don't have to have a tall hat and a black cat and a nose that nearly meets your bristly chin.

But no one spoke to him. Perhaps she'll come after dark, Sam thought, on her broomstick.

He was up in his room, doing his homework, when he heard his mother calling.

"What is it, Mum?" Sam said from the top of the stairs.

"I'm just going next door to borrow something and Dad's not back yet. Can you answer the phone if it rings?"

"OK," Sam said.

Five minutes later, it wasn't the phone that rang but the front door bell. Sam ran downstairs and opened the door. The moment he set eyes on the woman who stood there, he knew without doubt that she was a witch.

To be sure she had no hat nor cat, and her nose was normal and her chin smooth. In fact she was quite young and rather pretty, though her face was very brown and weatherbeaten. But in addition to a bag slung on her shoulder, containing wooden clothes-pegs and sprigs of heather, she was carrying a long-handled broomstick.

"Good evening, young sir," she said. "Is your mother at home?"

"No," said Sam. He took a deep breath and then he said, "Are you a witch?"

The young gypsy woman stared at him for a moment, and then her brown face broke into a smile.

"Is it the broomstick?" she said. "It's just the thing for sweeping up the autumn leaves, but I don't know about riding on it."

"But witches *can* fly, can't they?"

"So they say."

"What about warlocks? Can they?"

"Warlocks, is it?" said the gypsy. "Why do you ask, young sir?"

"Because," said Sam, "I am one."

"Are you indeed?" said the gypsy. "How do you know?"

And without hesitation – because somehow it seemed he must – Sam told her all the things that had happened since he had first read the story of the warlock who had got all he wanted by making up a few magic rhymes.

"I just say them," he told her, "and it happens."

"Like breaking your mother's washing-machine and your father's arm," said the gypsy woman.

"Yes, but good things too," Sam said. "The money, and Ben scoring that goal."

"Young sir," said the gypsy, putting down her bag of pegs and heather, and propping the broomstick against the wall, "give me your hand."

Ben held out his arm, and the gypsy took his right hand in hers, turned it palm uppermost and looked intently into it.

"You're to be lucky," she said, when at last she released it. "It might not have been so. It is dangerous to meddle with magic."

"Why?" said Sam. "Why is it dangerous?"

"Those who practise magic – warlocks like you, and witches —"

"Like you," put in Sam.

"... such people are, some say, in league with the Devil. There is evil in magic as well as good, and sometimes great harm can be done where none was meant. Will you take advice from a stranger?"

"Yes," said Sam. "I will."

"Stop," said the gypsy. "Stop now, young sir. Stop playing with fire before you are burned."

"But," said Sam, "you haven't told me – can warlocks fly? Could *I*?"

"Just suppose," said the gypsy, "that a boy of your age was to make up a magic rhyme about flying, and then jump on a broomstick and try to take off. What would happen?"

"He'd fly?" said Sam.

"Only birds," said the gypsy, "can fly. Like I said just now, don't meddle with magic, no matter what you think you are."

At that moment Sam's mother emerged from the house next door. Sam heard her saying goodbye, and soon she came through the gate and up the garden path.

"Clothes-pegs, my lady?" said the gypsy. "Lucky heather? Or a fine strong besom to sweep your leaves?"

"No, thank you," said Sam's mother. "We don't want anything."

"Oh, Mum," said Sam, "couldn't we have the broomstick? I'd sweep the leaves for you. Please, please, can we have it?"

Sam's mother looked narrowly at him. Then she looked at the gypsy, who said nothing but stood, smiling.

"How much is it?" she asked.

"To tell the truth, my lady," said the gypsy woman, "your son here has entertained me so politely that I would like him to have the besom, as a gift."

"No, no," said Sam's mother. "I couldn't possibly accept that."

If I do, she thought, the woman won't go till she's sold me every clothes-peg and heather sprig in that bag.

"I'll get my purse," she said.

When she came out again, the gypsy had shouldered her bag and Sam was already clutching the broomstick.

Sam's mother opened her purse. "Oh, dear," she said. "I've only got a five-pound note."

"That will do nicely, my lady," said the gypsy, taking it. "And here's a sprig of lucky heather for you, young sir," and then she turned and made off down the path.

Still carrying the broomstick, Sam ran to catch her up.

"Sorry," he said. "I didn't say thank you. What's your name?"

"Rose May."

"Well, thank you, Rose May. For the lucky heather.

And for the broomstick."

"Just don't try riding it," said Rose May.

"I won't. And thank you for your advice. I'll think about it."

"Think carefully, Sam," said the gypsy. "Time for you to forget your other name."

"What other name?"

"Warlock Watson."

Chapter 8
The Cypress

Like many boys of his age, Sam was mostly sensible but could be silly. The sensible side of him said, "Look, you've been warned – straight from the witch's mouth – to lay off warlockry or you may regret it." The silly side said, "OK, but how about one last magic rhyme before I retire?"

There's no knowing who might have won – sensible or silly – had it not been for Mr Hogg. Yes, it was Piggy who was in the middle of it all because of something he said in class the very next day.

"Who can tell me," he said, "what's special about next Wednesday?"

Everyone looked blank, so Piggy pointed to the calendar on the wall and said, "A week from today.

What's that?"

"The last day of October," someone said.

"Well, what's that?"

Ben's hand shot up.

"Well?"

"Hallowe'en, sir!"

"Right, Ben," said Mr Hogg. "I'd have expected *you* to answer that, Sam Watson."

"Why, sir?" said Sam nervously.

Oh, Lor'! Piggy's not going to give me away, is he? he thought.

"Because Hallowe'en is particularly Scottish in flavour, and you, like myself, have Scottish blood. You must read Robert Burns' poem about it. Tell me, someone, what happens at Hallowe'en?"

"Trick or treat, sir," someone said.

"Yes. What else?"

"You get a pumpkin," said a boy, "and hollow it out."

"And carve a face on it," said a girl, "and put a candle inside."

"Yes, yes," said Mr Hogg, "but what is it that's

supposed to happen on the night of Hallowe'en?"

"Witches!" cried several voices. "They all come out and fly about on their broomsticks."

"That's right," said Mr Hogg. "Witches, and warlocks too." He looked directly at Sam as he said this, and Sam could almost have sworn that he winked.

"You see," he went on, "in the old Celtic calendar, October 31st was the last night of the year, and on that night, so folk believed, the witches and warlocks held their wicked revels. For a witch, or a warlock, Hallowe'en is the most magical of all nights. Now we're not going to hold any wicked revels, but we *are* going to make Hallowe'en masks, and then next Wednesday evening you can each take your mask home to terrify your wretched parents and frighten your old grannies and scare your baby brothers and sisters to bits."

Throughout that last week of October Sam couldn't stop thinking about Hallowe'en. Even if he'd wanted to, he would have been continually reminded by the masks they were all busy making and the enormous pumpkin they were working on.

As it was, he couldn't get his teacher's words out of his head: "For a witch, or a warlock, Hallowe'en is the most magical of all nights."

And he, Sam Watson, was a warlock.

Next Wednesday he simply *must* make up one last magic spell, whatever Rose May might have said.

But what would it be? Something really big? To be given some very expensive present?

Come to that, why not magic up enough money to buy all the expensive things anyone could want?

Why, thought the silly Sam, I could be a self-made millionaire! But then the sensible Sam thought that that might be very difficult to explain, and anyway, he remembered hearing someone saying that money was the root of all evil.

By the morning of October 31st Sam had still not made up his mind what spell to say.

That afternoon the children put the finishing touches to their masks, and then they put them on. Piggy's pumpkin was all hollowed out, with a horrid face carved on it and a candle burning inside. The

scene in the classroom was really ghostly and weird.

It wasn't until he arrived back home from school that afternoon that Sam knew, suddenly and certainly, what he must do.

It was just as he turned into the front gate that the idea struck him. At one side of the gate there stood a solitary tall tree. It was an evergreen, a cypress, and for ages the Watsons had argued about it.

Mrs Watson wanted it cut down. "It blocks out all the light from the front room and from Sam's bedroom too," she said. "Great dark gloomy thing!"

But Mr Watson rather liked it. "Anyway," he said, "it would cost the earth to get a tree surgeon to remove it. The only way to fell it is right across the road and you'd have to get permission from the Council and heaven knows what."

But as Sam walked in that Hallowe'en afternoon, wearing his devilish-looking mask, he looked up at the tall cypress swaying to and fro. And then he remembered the story he had read, where the warlock had just put his hand against a tree and said a magic rhyme, and down it fell.

"That's it!" said Sam. "All the other things that have happened might just be chance. But if I can do this, then I really am a warlock. Mum wants it down anyway, I know, and it'll save Dad the expense of paying someone to do it."

When it was dark, Sam went out by himself into the little front garden. He was wearing his mask and straddling Rose May's broomstick, so that the bundle of birch twigs stuck out behind him like a tail. Round the garden he went, seven times (for he knew that seven was a magic number), and then he put down the broomstick and went up to the cypress tree.

First he made sure that his father wasn't back from work yet. No, there was no car parked outside. Then he looked up and down the road to be certain nothing was coming. Then he put his hand against the trunk of the cypress and cried above the noise of the wind,

"Tree so tall
Fall, tree, fall."

Nothing happened.

Sam went to bed feeling very disappointed. He had

been so sure that this last magic rhyme would work, on Hallowe'en of all nights. Why hadn't it?

As usual he slept like a log, but when he woke next morning, he noticed something odd. His room seemed lighter.

Sam got out of bed and went to the window. The cypress tree was down, lying across the road, and there was a police car parked not far away, and there were workmen putting up DIVERSION signs, and all sorts of activity.

Sam dressed in a hurry and ran downstairs and outside. His mother and father were already there.

"The tree's down!" he said.

"It was the gale," his mother said. "It was blowing a terrible gale in the night."

"Don't tell me you slept through it," his father said. "It was blowing like all the devils in hell."

"Was anyone hurt?" Sam asked.

"No one was hurt," said his father, "but something else was. Have a look."

So Sam went past them, through the gate and out on to the pavement, and there, under the great dark mass of the fallen tree, he saw the Watsons' car. Squashed flat.

Chapter 9
The Final Rhyme

I did that! thought Sam in horror. They said it was the gale that blew the tree down but they don't realize what I did. I don't know what time it fell, but just think – Dad might have been in the car! Rose May was right. She said sometimes great harm can be done. I'm never going to meddle with magic again. Never!

He was late into school and had to explain why to Mr Hogg.

"Smashed your father's car, did it?" said Piggy. "I hope he's properly insured."

"I expect so," Sam said. "He works for an insurance company."

Throughout the day he became steadily more miserable at the thought of what had happened and what might have happened. By the time school ended he felt that he simply must tell someone, that he must get it off his chest. He waited behind when the class was dismissed.

Mr Hogg looked up from his desk to see him standing there.

"Off you go then, Sam," he said.

"Please, sir," Sam said, "can I tell you something?"

"Of course. What is it?"

"I did it, sir."

"Did what?"

"I made that tree fall down. I didn't know it would smash our car, but I made it fall. You see, I *am* a warlock."

Mr Hogg looked narrowly at Sam, but there was a kindly light in his small piggy eyes.

"Sam," he said, "a warlock you may be, but that tree was blown down by the gale. What happened is not your fault. Now push off, and stop worrying."

But it was my fault and I can't stop worrying, said Sam to himself as he trudged gloomily homewards. I wish I'd never read that book. I wish I'd never made up any rhymes. I wish I wasn't a warlock.

Outside his house everything had been cleared up. Only a gaping hole showed where the cypress had stood. The tree had been cut up and removed, and the wreck of the car had been carted off to the breakers' yard. Sam's father had been given a lift to work by a friend.

"You look as if you've eaten a lemon," Sam's mother said when he came in. "Cheer up! I've got some good news."

You can't have won another five hundred pounds, Sam thought. Not without my help.

"What news?" he said.

"Well," said Mrs Watson, "it's lucky that your father knows so much about car insurance. He's rung up to say that the company he insured the car with is going to pay us quite a lot of money."

"How much?" said Sam.

"Never you mind. Enough to buy a new car, anyway."

"A new one?"

"Yes. Dad thinks we'll be able to afford the latest model in that range. So, you see, it's an ill wind that blows nobody any good."

Sam went up to his bedroom and shut the door. He stood and looked at the reflection in the mirror, at his gloomy face. And as he looked, and as he thought over what his mother had just told him, his face began to brighten.

A brand-new car! "You're to be lucky," Rose May had said. How right she was! And how good her advice was.

Sam sat down on his bed and began to think. After a long while he stood up and, slowly and clearly, he said,

"Now Warlock Watson is no more.

Whatever I could do before,

I never will again. My power

Is vanished from this very hour.

An ordinary boy I am.

This is the final spell of Sam."

Then he felt suddenly very happy.

Then he felt suddenly very hungry.

"What's for tea, Mum?" shouted Sam as he hurtled downstairs. "I'm starving!"

Another fantastic Young Hippo
from the same author:

What Sadie
Saw

Chapter 1

The First Pictures

It was shortly before her eighth birthday that Sadie first realized her extraordinary gift.

She could see into the future.

There was no warning of it. She went to bed one night a perfectly normal girl, and she woke up knowing – with absolute certainty – two things about the next day.

She lay in bed thinking about this. In the crook of her arm was her favourite old toy, a very battered and threadbare camel called Abdul. Abdul's ears had fallen off and his two humps were all soft and floppy but his beady black eyes were still bright as Sadie told him what had happened.

She told Abdul everything, always had, but never

before anything as exciting as this.

"Listen, Abdul," she said, "and I'll tell you two things about today, two things that I *know* are going to happen. I've got pictures in my mind. One's got something to do with rain – a storm of rain, a thunderstorm, I dare say. And the other is about money – about me finding some money, I think. I'm absolutely sure in my mind about both these things."

Abdul, as was his habit, said nothing.

"I'm only telling all this to you," said Sadie, "not to the rest of the family. It's a secret between you and me, understand?" and the old camel nodded his head up and down several times, possibly because Sadie had hold of his neck and was waggling it.

Sadie was the eldest of the three Makepeace children. Carl was four and a half, and there was a baby called Julia.

At breakfast, Sadie watched her mother ladling food into Julia's gaping, birdlike mouth and said, "Mum, are you going to have another baby?"

"Steady on!" said Mrs Makepeace. "Julia's only ten months old."

"I don't mean straight away," Sadie said. "I mean, are you going to have another one some time?"

"No!" said Mr Makepeace firmly.

"I don't know," said his wife. "And hurry up with your breakfast or we'll be late for school."

Sadie poured milk on to her Rice Krispies and listened to them snapping and crackling and popping. You may not know, Mum, she thought, what's going to happen in the future, but if you wait a while I'll probably be able to tell you if Carl and Julia and I are going to have another brother or sister; at the moment I'm only looking one day ahead, but you never know, I may get better at it.

The day started fine and warm with clear skies, but as she skipped around the playground at morning break, Sadie thought she heard a distant rumble. It was hard to be sure, with all the shouting and yelling the children were making, but halfway through the next lesson there was a sudden dazzle of lightning and then a great clap of thunder that made everyone jump. After that, the rain came down in torrents.

And when school ended, and the three Makepeace

children were on their way home with their mother, Sadie suddenly saw something shining at the edge of the pavement, and she bent and picked up a one-pound coin. That evening she told her camel all about it.

"It all happened," she said, "exactly as I had fore-seen, Abdul Pasha."

("Pasha", she had found in a book, was a title given to very important Turkish people. She saw no reason why Abdul should not be a Turkish camel, and he was certainly a very important person.)

"How odd it is," Sadie went on, "to think that when I wake up tomorrow morning, I shall foresee some more things."

But she was wrong. When she woke, she found she had absolutely no knowledge about the day ahead except that it was Saturday.

Funny, Sadie thought. How could I have been so certain about those two things happening? Was it just a fluke?

For ten days or more it seemed that it was, but then one morning Sadie woke up with that same feeling of certainty about what would happen that day.

It wasn't a feeling about something natural, like a thunderstorm, or something nice, like finding a one-pound coin. It was definitely a nasty feeling; something nasty was going to happen, to someone in the family, she didn't know who, she didn't know what.

But once again there was the clearest picture in her mind, a picture of something dripping – drip, drip, drip – down on to the floor. They were bright red, these drips. And they weren't tomato sauce.

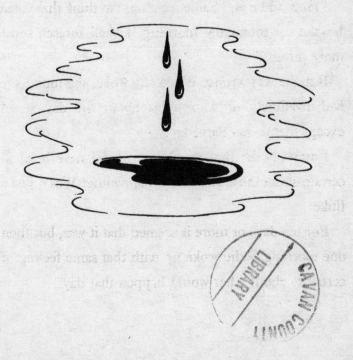